To This AMAZING Person:

Date:

From:

KEEPSAKE MEMORIES
AND
Miracles
BOOK

RoyalKIND

RoyalKIND®
Winterville, NC

For permission request, email the Publisher at
encouragesomeone@RoyalKIND.org
Quantity sales. Special discounts are available on quantity purchases by corporations, associations, and others. For details, contact the publisher at the email address above.

ISBN: 978-1-7338600-5-5   First Edition: 1 2 3 4 5 6 7 8 9 10

Contents

09   FAVORITE QUOTES AND FACTS

35   MEMORIES I WANT TO KEEP

61   HOLIDAY TRADITIONS AND IDEAS

87   DEEP THOUGHTS RANDOM THOUGHTS

111   TO BE'S TO DO'S

139   INVITATIONS TO TAKE THE TIME

151   MY MIRACLES

You are **Royal**:
Chosen, Loved, Approved.

You are equipped to be **Kind**:
You can change someone's world for the
better in an instant.

QUOTES & FACTS

Journal your favorite quotes and facts. They can tell you a lot about yourself.

They're also great conversation starters.

MEMORIES

You are blessed
beyond measure.
Every single day is a
day you should treasure.

**You can be a masterpiece
and a work in progress
at the same time.**

HOLIDAY TRADITIONS AND IDEAS

Choose to see the good.

When you can't see the light at the end of the tunnel, you must choose to LIGHT it yourself.

Deep thoughts. 

Random thoughts.

You are unique. You are not like everyone else.

So, write your thoughts down, and encourage someone else to write theirs too!

TO BE'S.
TO DO'S.

You were born for such
a time as this.

**People won't remember what you
accomplished; they'll remember
how you made them feel.**

DO SOMETHING TODAY

THAT YOUR FUTURE SELF WILL

THANK YOU FOR.

Let the ideas on the
following pages help you
start your journey.

Journal the
Miracles that happen.

IDEA:

Be a friend, listen.
Who should you be intentional
with today?

Take time for coffee or lunch
with a friend or loved one.

IDEA:

Go make it happen.
What would you do if you knew
you would not fail?

How to Live It:

Take the risk.

IDEA:

The fruit comes after
you plant the seed.
Who should you be patient with today?

HOW TO LIVE IT:

Give free hugs and positive advice today, even when it's not easy.

IDEA:

Your response has power. What areas in your life need your response of kindness? Work, family, friends?

HOW TO LIVE IT:

Share a smile or a compliment
with someone today.
It could change their world
for the better in an instant.

IDEA:

People matter.
Who should you "Take the Time"
to get to know?

Strike up a conversation with people that cross your path today.

Remember always:

You are a Masterpiece.
There is nothing from
your past or in your future
that will ever change that.

My *Miracles*

Great and Small.

Write them down on the next few pages
as a reminder to be thankful
for them all.

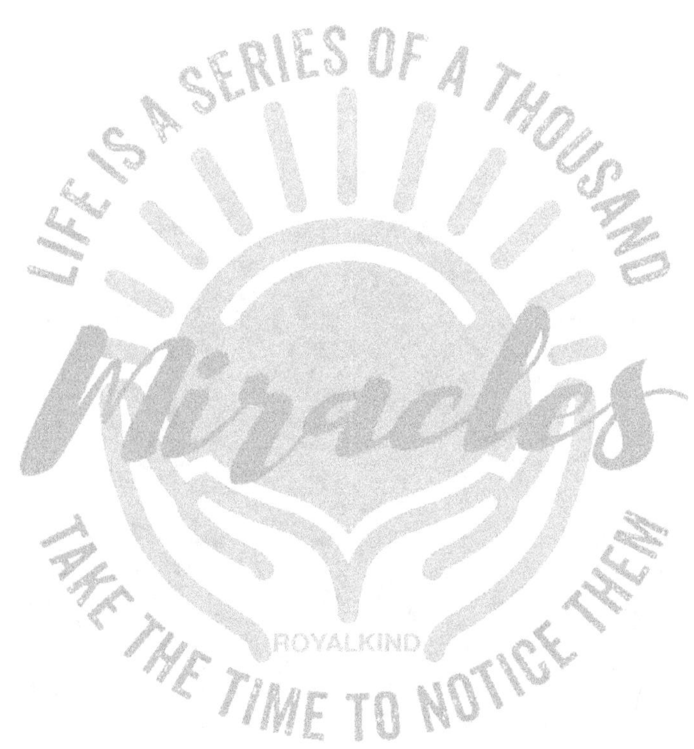

You are Royalty!

You have the power to change someone's world for the better in an instant.

Check out our
RoyalKIND WayofLife *Journal.*

- Be inspired to learn who you were created to be.

- Be challenged to create new habits of kindness.

- Learn how to see and focus on the beauty in this world.

Go to RoyalKIND.org